FAMILIES

SUSAN KUKLIN

HYPERION BOOKS FOR CHILDREN

NEW YORK

For information address Hyperion Books for Children,

114 Fifth Avenue, New York, New York 10011-5690.

Printed in Singapore

First Edition

1 3 5 7 9 10 8 6 4 2

This book is set in 15-point Deepdene.

Reinforced binding

ISBN 0-7868-0822-5

Library of Congress Cataloging-in-Publication Data on file.

Visit www.hyperionbooksforchildren.com

A special thanks to friends and colleagues behind the scenes: my editor, Donna Bray;

art director, Christine Kettner; Caroline Ward at the Ferguson Library in Stamford, Connecticut;

Dr. Louise Friedman; Lisa Son; and Fran Katzman. Three cheers to Marshall Norstein, pal, partner, and

confidant, who helps me make photographs.

This book has a fairy godmother, and her name is Emilyn Garrick.

She is a perfect teacher at P.S. 11 in Manhattan.

Emilyn introduced me to many families.

Her students love her a lot—and so do I.

Dear Readers:

To make this book, I talked with many wonderful children between the ages of four and fourteen about their families. They told me what it's like to live with brothers and sisters, and what it's like to be an only child. They described living with just one parent and living in a larger, extended family. They discussed adoption, divorce, race, special needs, and more. For some children, religion plays a major part in their lives. For others, the customs and culture of their ethnic heritage take center stage. What they all have in common is that they feel safe and loved. And they want you to know about them.

I worked with each family through a series of interviews and one long photography session. The children decided what should be included about their lives. Sometimes they chose to talk to me in private—no parents allowed. Other times, these same kids invited their siblings and parents to join in.

Not only did the children direct the text for *Families*, they had a clear view of how they wanted their home life portrayed visually. They chose the settings and poses for the photographs. They decided what everyone—including the grown-ups—would wear. They brought along toys, dolls, real or stuffed pets, or musical instruments. One of the first things many of them did was show me their family scrapbook. I saw wonderful photographs of their earlier years, ancestors, and people and places important to their lives. Following their lead, I asked each child to lend one special photograph from their family album to help describe who they are.

Knowing these children and their families has been a joyful experience for me. Everyone was friendly and helpful and fun. It was hard to leave their warm and happy homes. I wish I could have included even more families. I wish I could have included yours as well.

It is my hope that the children in *Families* will inspire you to think about your own life and the family that makes you special.

Susan Kuklin

FAMILIES

Ben: *Just Me*

When I come home—say, from a sleepover or something—I feel happy because home is a very nice place to be. I've got my own room. I've got my parents' undivided attention. If I have a problem, I go to my parents. I have my parents all to myself because I'm an only child. Sometimes I am sad about that, but usually I'm kind of relieved. Most of my friends have brothers and sisters, and most of them tell me that they really get on their nerves.

This a picture of my *papou's* grandfather and grandmother from Greece. If my *yia yia* (grandmother) and my *papou* (grandfather) stayed in Greece, my parents wouldn't have gotten married and I wouldn't exist. That's a weird thing. God got us here.

We live in a big apartment house, and there's a playground on floor two. I can go outside, usually whenever I want. I don't feel lonely because I live close to many of my friends and I can see them a lot. My friends act like brothers and sisters.

My mom's an actor and my dad's a stage manager. The good thing about Mom's job is I get to see her performances. In most of her shows she's pretty funny. I like that.

My mom's been on the road for a while. She comes home Sunday night and stays till Tuesday. This is her third job in a row, and Dad's going to start his fourth job in a row, and I don't get to spend enough time with them. It doesn't make me angry, but . . . Oh, I don't know how to describe it.

The good thing about Dad's job is, he is home until about noon. On weekend mornings we go out and play baseball. We also make things together. The best thing we made was my bunk bed. Dad constructs my costumes for Halloween. I've been a Bionicle, and the Grim Reaper. Since we make so much stuff, when I grow up I want to be a carpenter.

I enjoy being by myself. I make up stories. It would be hard to do that with a bunch of brothers and sisters around making noise. You need peace in order to do that.

Noah, Morgan, and Sage:
That Voice

MORGAN: I wonder about what's going to happen when I grow older and Sage grows older. And what she's going to look like? I think she's going to be pretty tall. I think I will, too. I'm only seven and I'm taller than almost everybody in the class.

SAGE: Me and my big sister share a room. We share toys. And stencils. And makeup.

MORGAN: Noah is my big brother. He usually ignores me a lot. My brother and sister never want to play with me.

SAGE and NOAH: Yes, we do!

NOAH: When I was really young I wanted a sister, but I think that was a mistake. Now I want a brother, an older brother, who can drive a car.

I have a lot of fun with my sisters, but sometimes they get on my nerves. Other times we just have fun and they don't get on my nerves at all.

NOAH: This is a picture of Ruth Geyer. She was Dad's grandmother and our great-grandmother. She was the daughter of Penelope Geyer, a Mescolaro Indian. We've heard lots of stories about how Penelope found her way to Harlem and married a German-Jewish man named Geyer.

MORGAN: My family cheers me up when I feel sad. My dad does it most. He tells me funny stories.

NOAH: We listen to our parents. They have that voice. If I'm doing something my mom doesn't like, she'll say, "Okay, do what you want." The voice makes me want to do what they told me, because they are right most of the time. Mom said, "You shouldn't play with your Game Boy outside." But I took it out anyway. My Game Boy absolutely broke the day she said that.

My parents let us have fun, but they always put homework and grades and education first. Me? I want to be a children's book writer. I write fiction. My one book is named *A Water Molecule*. It's about a kid who can turn into water.

My favorite thing is to tell my mom and dad about my books. My dad edits them. My parents are very smart.

MORGAN: My mom comes back from work at around six or seven. We always wait and have dinner as a family. My mom, my dad, or my babysitter makes dinner. We like to eat together.

Osamu and Musashi:
The Wonderer and the Creative Wise Guy

OSAMU: Kids have different things about their families, some big and some small. Our big thing is the fact that our mom is Japanese and our dad is American. And because of that we get to do a lot of you-don't-know-how-lucky-you-are things.

MUSASHI: Because we're half Japanese, we get two passports. We get to go to Japan every summer to visit our grand-mother. We get to speak both English and Japanese.

OSAMU: When we are here we celebrate American holidays, and when we are in Japan we celebrate Japanese holidays.

This is Mom and Dad's wedding picture.

MUSASHI: In Japan, one of the most important things is manners. You have to sit correctly at the table. You have to hold chopsticks correctly. People aren't so strict about that in America.

OSAMU: I'm two years and a little bit older than Musashi. I'm responsible for him. I take him to school. I drag him along on the subway. Sometimes he gets on my nerves, but usually he's a really nice guy, a great person to be next to.

MUSASHI: Osamu's the guy who understands another person's point of view well. He's a good brother.

OSAMU: I'm a creative wise guy. I'm good at making up some stuff. I say funny stuff at just the right time.

MUSASHI: I have all these wonders: I wonder if there will be world peace. I wonder if there is such a thing as levitation. I wonder if there is such a thing as heaven or hell. I wonder if there's any other intelligent life-form out in the universe. I wonder if it's possible to go at the speed of light. If it's possible to reach Andromeda.

OSAMU: 'Cause he's a fourth-grade genius, that's why. He was doing multiplication when he was in first grade. You should be thankful to us, Musashi. *Thankful!* Dad, Mom, and I taught you.

MUSASHI: I'm a lot more like my mom, and Osamu is a lot more like Dad. Dad's good at writing. Osamu is a very good poet.

OSAMU: Dancing is my big thing. Tango. Waltz. Fox-trot. Swing. I try to teach Mom and Musashi meringue, but it's not working. Musashi's good at music.

MUSASHI: I play the piano, like my dad. We do different music. My father is rock, blues, jazz. I'm classical, ragtime.

OSAMU: We're a fun-loving, culturally mixed-up family. Mixed is more fun.

Kira and Matias: *A Fishy Conversation*

KIRA: When we're outdoors, Mommy needs a whole bottle of sunscreen to protect her skin. I need three quarters. Matias needs only half. And Daddy only needs a quarter. He never burns.

Daddy and I make up the biggest stories. Next comes Matias. Mommy never tells made-up stories at all. Daddy calls these "fish stories."

My mom was born in Germany. My dad was supposed to be born in a hospital, but he was in a big hurry. He was born outside, in front of a movie theater in New York City.

MATIAS: My sister was in a hurry, too. She was born at home, here, on this very couch. I was born at the hospital, like most kids. I'd say we're a non-normal family.

KIRA: I like the fact that instead of getting fish in the store, me and Mom go fishing in the creek next to our house.

MATIAS: That's a fish story! The only thing we catch in our creek is tadpoles.

KIRA: No, we catch bigger fish. In the swimming hole down the road we catch frogs and other specimens like leaves and stones and mushrooms, and other things. Then we go home and look at them under our microscope.

MATIAS: One time I caught, unexpectedly, a bug-bug that looked

KIRA: I'm holding a net to catch frogs. On my brother's back is his book bag with all our supplies. And behind us is our wonderful waterfall.

14

like a little shrimp. It was cute.

KIRA: It was cool because we had never seen it before. I wondered what it was. We looked it up in the book. It was a crayfish. My dad said, "That's an excellent catch." After a few days we let it go in our creek.

MATIAS: We always put back our specimens.

KIRA: When I let him go I felt sad because I was in love with it. I had named it Crayfish.

MATIAS: In the night my favorite thing is bats. My favorite instrument is the piano.

KIRA: My favorite instrument is the violin, but mostly I like to read and write. Another thing about me is I never argue with my parents. I stay calm.

MATIAS: Fish, fish, fish, fish.

KIRA: Matias is another story. He argues all the time. I try to help him. I try to keep him calm. I help him with his homework.

MATIAS: I don't have any homework.

KIRA: Well, you're going to get homework and I'm going to help you.

Ella: *We're Alike and Like It*

Sometimes when I go to the park with my two dads, someone comes up to me and says, "Who are those guys? Is one your father and one your friend?" I say, "No, those are both my fathers." Then they might ask me a lot of questions like, "What happened to your mother?" Well, I was adopted. It would be kind a hard to imagine not having two dads. I've been with them since I was three months old. They're all I know. I call them Daddy Stephen and Daddy Frank, or sometimes I call them just Stephen or Frank.

Stephen usually gets me ready for school and Frank puts me to bed at night. In the morning I find a letter from Frank. He tells me there is a smoothie in the refrigerator and to have a good day. He signs it with a drawing of a little smiley face. It lets me know he loves me.

Last summer, I went to an all-girls sleep-away camp. We learned there was a weekend for moms only. When I heard the word "moms," I was a little bit worried I would be the only person without a mom. Daddy Frank came up with a solution, "Let's call Hazel." Hazel had been my babysitter since I was a baby. She's part of our family. On the first day of Moms Weekend almost everyone else's mom got there early. But where was Hazel? Then I saw her coming up the hill. Daddy Frank had driven Hazel to camp. He went to a hotel till the next day, when the whole family could come.

This is a picture of chubby me soon after my dads adopted me.

Another thing about us is me and Stephen are black and Frank's white. Once, we had an ice cream party. It's kind of silly, but when I saw cartons of

vanilla and chocolate ice cream, it reminded me of Stephen and me and Frank. Sometimes my family reminds me of an Oreo cookie.

Some people ask questions about how we are different. I'd rather they ask how we're alike.

Verona and Leona: *Sisters Who Fight and Love, but Mostly Love*

LEONA: Our family is my sister, my mom, my dad, and me. Me and my sister were born here and my mom and dad were born in Trinidad. We have a big sister, Melanie. She lives in Trinidad.

VERONA: Before me and Leona were born, Mom and Dad worked all day. There was no one to watch Melanie, so Mom sent her to live with our grandma, Mom's mom. We only get to see our sister on holidays, like Easter and Christmas, and summer vacation.

LEONA: When we don't have Melanie around we miss her so much. She left her toy dog here for us to remember her.

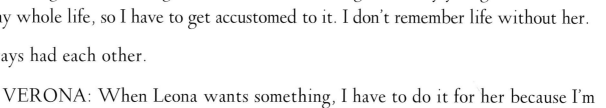

We love this picture because we're little and our big sister is with us.

VERONA: When me and Leona play together, it's really hard sometimes. I'm older and her games are boring for me. Somehow I manage. She's my younger sister and I will be with her for my whole life, so I have to get accustomed to it. I don't remember life without her.

LEONA: We've always had each other.

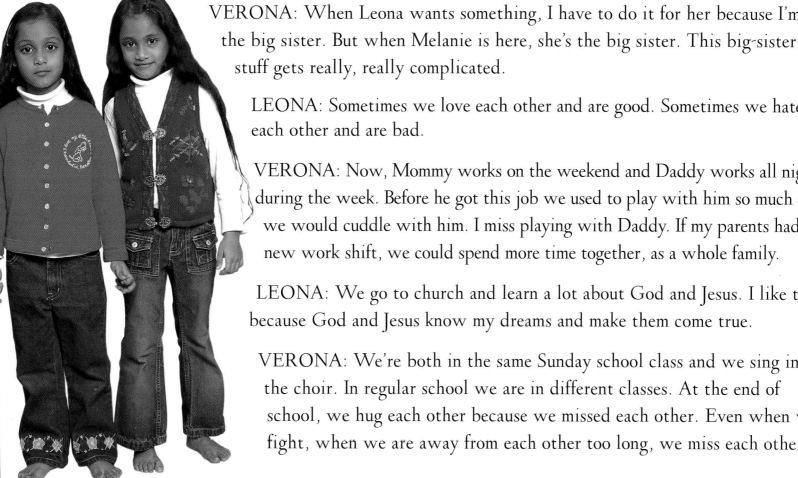

VERONA: When Leona wants something, I have to do it for her because I'm the big sister. But when Melanie is here, she's the big sister. This big-sister stuff gets really, really complicated.

LEONA: Sometimes we love each other and are good. Sometimes we hate each other and are bad.

VERONA: Now, Mommy works on the weekend and Daddy works all night during the week. Before he got this job we used to play with him so much and we would cuddle with him. I miss playing with Daddy. If my parents had a new work shift, we could spend more time together, as a whole family.

LEONA: We go to church and learn a lot about God and Jesus. I like that because God and Jesus know my dreams and make them come true.

VERONA: We're both in the same Sunday school class and we sing in the choir. In regular school we are in different classes. At the end of school, we hug each other because we missed each other. Even when we fight, when we are away from each other too long, we miss each other.

Joshua, Ashley, and Kati:
A Sleepover with Your Best Friend Forever

ASHLEY: Kati and I are twins.

KATI: Sometimes our friends just say Ashley-Kati so they don't have to tell us apart.

ASHLEY: Our family can tell us apart, but other kids can't. I think we're different. My eyes are bigger than Kati's. Her face is round, but mine is not.

JOSHUA: When I was an only child, I wasn't a social person. And then when I was five, in kindergarten, my sisters were born. I hated them a lot because they were, like, crying and really loud. And they pulled my hair and stuff. When they grew up it was easier. I taught them how to play games and now it's really fun.

ASHLEY: But I still like to touch his hair.

We live with Grandpa, Grandma [they're out of town right now], Mommy, Daddy, and our big brother, Joshua. We were born in New Jersey and our parents were born in Korea. We call our grandpa *Harabughi*. It means "grand father" in Korean. And we call Grandma *Halmoni*.

JOSHUA: *Harabughi* makes us breakfast, eggs, bacon, and a bagel. Every meal before we

ASHLEY– KATI: This picture was taken at Mommy's sixth birthday party in Korea. She's with her little sister, her mommy and daddy, and her *halmoni*. We like it because she was six then and we are six now.

eat, we pray to God for all the things that He gave us. When me and my sisters pray, we do it in English because we can't say it in Korean.

ASHLEY: We sing a lot of Korean songs. Grandpa and Mommy taught us.

JOSHUA: We show respect for our elders by bowing when we say hello, bye, and thank you.

KATI: And we don't interrupt when the grown-ups are speaking.

JOSHUA: My hobby is drawing. I use my fingers, my head, and my imagination.

ASHLEY: I draw things that are my own, not copying. I like having my imagination do it. If we like our drawings, we give them to our mom.

KATI: Me and Ashley share one big bed. And one time we had a TV in our room—

JOSHUA: But my parents took it away because they watched twenty-four–seven. Now they sing to each other. It's so loud. They never whisper.

ASHLEY: At night we don't read because Joshua tells us funny stories that he makes up.

JOSHUA: For them, it's like having a sleepover with your best friend forever! They're double trouble, double fun.

Yaakov, Leah, Miriam, and Asher: *Twins and Family Matters*

ASHER: In our family there's Mommy; Daddy; my twin sister, Miriam; my older sister, Leah; me; and my big brother, Yaakov.

MIRIAM: The first language I know is English. The second language I'm learning is Hebrew. Yiddish is the third lanuguage. Then there's this funny language that me and my twin brother made up. I'll tell you, but don't laugh. I say, *hammacamamakukka cokka*.

ASHER: I answer, *smork*.

MIRIAM: Even though Asher and I are twins, and even though we have our own language, we are very different. We don't have the same thoughts.

ASHER: I save up candies.

MIRIAM: This picture was taken before me and my brother were born. It was when my older sister and my older brother were in Israel with my bubby on my father's side. They are in front of the Wailing Wall, a holy place in Israel.

MIRIAM: I eat mine right away. I wear a skirt.

ASHER: And I wear pants.

MIRIAM: He wears something under his shirt called *tzitzit* and he wears a yarmulke on his head.

ASHER: The *tzitzit* reminds us of all the kindnesses we do, like being nice to our parents and giving money to poor people.

MIRIAM: I wear skirts that cover my knees and long-sleeved shirts. There's a rule that you have to be modest. We're Jewish.

ASHER: And we all go to a Jewish school.

MIRIAM: We pray at least three times a day. Then, before we go to sleep, we say an extra little prayer. We think of such a beautiful day we had and thank G-d for it.

ASHER: Because we're Jewish, we have things we're not allowed to do.

We're not allowed to go to restaurants and eat whatever we want. We have to have food that is kosher. Kosher means food that is specially prepared according to Jewish law. We're not allowed to mix meat and milk. We're not allowed to eat pigs or seafood.

MIRIAM: If you're not married you don't have to cover your hair. But our mother is married, so she wears either a hat or a wig to cover her hair.

YAAKOV: People might think that with all the restrictions, our religion stops us from enjoying life. But I feel that these restrictions help us enjoy life.

Shareef and Aly:
Different and the Same

SHAREEF: My mom's name is Ola and my dad's is Mahmoud. My brother is Aly, he's eight. I'm Shareef. We were born here, but our parents were born in Egypt. We're Muslims.

ALY: Our family, we do different things than other people.

SHAREEF: Our parents speak Arabic at home. My brother has trouble with Arabic, but is good in English. I'm good in both.

ALY: We pray five times a day.

SHAREEF: This picture was taken in Cairo, in Egypt, when we visited my grandmother and grandfather and my cousins and my uncle. This is at a special village for tourists. My dad's dressed as King Tut. My mother is King Tut's wife, and me and my brother are their sons.

SHAREEF: Since we go to a public school, we wait to pray when we come home.

ALY: We eat different foods than other people. We eat halal food. It's like the kosher food the Jewish people eat. We would never eat pork.

SHAREEF: We don't wear shoes in the house 'cause we don't want to let the outside dirt inside.

ALY: But some things we do are just like other people. I build rocket ships with my dad and play tickle with my mom. Our parents do everything for us.

SHAREEF: Sometimes I help Mom cook. My favorite food is Chinese. But Mommy makes Egyptian food. Mostly I like the desserts the best. My favorite dessert is *konafa*. It's made with shredded wheat and nuts and sugar.

ALY: Our big holiday is Ramadan. In Ramadan you can only eat when it's dark. When the sun comes up and the birds start singing, we stop eating. Ramadan lasts a whole month. 'Cause I'm too young to fast all day, my mom brings a tray of food in my bedroom when it's still dark. Sometimes I need to eat at snack time.

ALY: This year Mommy went on a pilgrimage to Mecca. That's called *hajj* in Arabic. Before she went, she didn't wear a head scarf. In Mecca, she said she got a feeling in her heart. And she now wears a head scarf for modesty. And to show her respect for God.

Maisie: *Three and a Half Days Each*

When Mommy and Daddy got divorced, I decided to stay half the time with Mommy and half the time with Daddy.

My mommy is Kara. I live with her half of Sunday, Wednesday, Thursday, and Friday. Daddy is John. I live with Daddy, his girlfriend, Erin, and our cat, Apu, Saturday, half of Sunday, Monday, and Tuesday.

When I'm here, my mommy wakes me up. When I'm at my other house, my daddy wakes me. Here, Mommy makes breakfast. And in the other house, Daddy makes breakfast. I get dressed by myself, but Mommy or Daddy does my hair.

They both help me with my homework. They both tickle me.

Mommy and Daddy make dinner, but they cook different things. Mommy makes fish and vegetables. Daddy makes vegetarian patties and string beans usually.

I have separate clothes so I don't have to take a suitcase with me. I have two toothbrushes, two different toothpastes, more than two nighties, but only one pair of glasses. I have more than one game at each house. I have art supplies in each house. At Mommy's I sleep with my doll, Maggie, and at Daddy's I usually sleep with my teddy bear, Emma.

On Friday night with Mommy, we have Shabbat. We light candles and say prayers. We celebrate Hanukkah together. We wait till we see the first three stars in the sky. Then we light a menorah. And then I get a present. Usually I celebrate Christmas with my dad. We have a Christmas tree and I open presents Christmas morning.

In this picture I am two years old, with my Grandma G. It comes from Grandma G's memory book. Mommy and I made it so I could remember her. She died when I was three and a half. I loved her very much.

On my birthday, Mommy, Daddy, Erin, and Mommy's parents celebrate with me.

Sometimes I feel sad that my parents are divorced. They say it's okay to say I'm sad. They understand. I can talk about it to both Mommy and Daddy. If there's something I can't talk about, I write it in my diary. It's only for me.

Even though it's sometimes hard, I know I will always have two parents who love me and take care of me.

Lily and Jacob: *So Lucky*

LILY: I have two moms, one little brother, whose name is Jacob, and a Siamese cat with long hair whose name is Sushi. One of my moms is Jennie and the other one's Lucy. We call Jennie "Mommy" and we call Lucy "Mama."

JACOB: My sister's a dancer. I'm an artist.

LILY: My moms teach at our school. One boy came up and asked, "Did you just call Lucy 'Mom'?" I said, "That's my mom." And he said, "I thought Jennie was your mom." I said, "I have two moms." And he said, *"You are so lucky!"*

JACOB: In our school the parents come to help the teachers during lunch and recess. One week Mommy helps and the next week Mama helps.

LILY: Mommy teaches dance. Every morning, before breakfast, we all drive to school together. We play music and sing. I sing musicals or Avril Lavigne. Mama is the teacher's teacher. We sometimes eat our cereal right in her private office. Our best friends come, too. We call this the Breakfast Club.

JACOB: I like having a big sister. Yesterday she did everything that I wanted.

LILY: Yesterday it was your birthday.
It's fun having a little brother, but sometimes he's a little bit annoying. Sometimes I just want to be by myself. When that happens, I open Mama's umbrella and make a tent.

28

This picture was taken with our friends on Super Saturday.

I turn a flashlight on and read, or play with my stuffed animals in there.

JACOB: And I look everywhere for Lily.

LILY: Every weekend our friends get together at one house for Super Saturday. On that day we do all sorts of things. We go to the movies. We go to the park. We do projects. And that gives the other parents time off. When I go to soccer, though, my moms and Jacob always come.

JACOB: Sometimes Mama watches Lily and Mommy and I play kick-the-ball. But we don't go far because we want to watch Lily play.

LILY: When I don't want to sleep, I ask my moms questions:

What birds like water?
Who is the Lord?
What happens if the ocean overflows with rain?
How old is Nana?
Does our country have kings and queens?

I like having two mommies because they are really nice moms. I don't just like them, I love them.

Chris, Louie, and Adam:
Three Special Brothers

CHRIS: My mother is a loving mother who knows how to cook very well. My father is a father who cares and wants us to do our best. My little brother, Adam, is a ball of fire with too much energy. Louie is a calm type. And me? I'm a big brother. I'm a curious person.

LOUIE: I'm Emilio. Everyone calls me Louie. Chris is a good brother. Adam is little bit nice. He talks back to us. Me? I'm good.

CHRIS: Louie may seem a little special, but he's special in a good way, not in a bad way. He was born with a condition called Down syndrome. I read a book about it. When he was born, instead of having twenty-six chromosomes, he has twenty-seven. People who have it learn a little slower than us.

ADAM: Louie is a happy person. He does everything that other people do. Everything.

CHRIS: Almost everything.

ADAM: I ask my mom questions about him, like, will Louie ever go to the same school that I do? Will Louie learn to read?

CHRIS: And Mom says, "Louie would get there sooner or later... he doesn't learn as fast as you."

CHRIS: This is our favorite picture. Three brothers and our grandma. Sometimes we call her Grandma and sometimes we call her Abuela—that's the word for "grandma" in Spanish.

30

LOUIE: I go to a special school. I'm learning to read.

CHRIS: Louie's condition doesn't hold us back. Basically we do what other families do.

LOUIE: We play games. Baseball. Dodgeball. We never fight.

CHRIS: Oh, yes we do.

LOUIE: Adam teases me.

ADAM: I tease him when he doesn't want to play with me. He teases back.

CHRIS: Then Adam will get mad. Me? I'm just sitting there.

ADAM: My mom, she's from the Dominican Republic, and my dad's family's from Puerto Rico. In my house we mostly speak English.

CHRIS: Our parents speak Spanish when they don't want us to know something. But I understand it.

LOUIE: I can say *si*. I can say *siéntate*, "sit down."

CHRIS: Mom mostly cooks Spanish food. She taught Dad the basics, and then he started experimenting on his own. He makes the best pork chops.

ADAM: And my favorite: rice and *salchichas*, little sausages in a can.

LOUIE: I like everything.

Carmen, Jared, Katie, and Hassan:
Loud and Big

KATIE: My mom is from Ecuador. My dad's family came from Germany and England a long time ago. Our family is loud and big.

CARMEN: I don't think about the different cultures in our family much. Here everybody is the same. Well, my mom's side is more crazy, and my dad's side is more calm.

HASSAN: I'm adopted. I was born in Africa, in Sierra Leone. I spoke two languages, Temne and Krio. Where I lived there was no electricity. I slept on a mat on the floor. I had only one blanket and no clothes. When I was getting adopted, Dad and I traveled almost all around the world.

KATIE: When Mom and Dad brought Hassan home I didn't understand him at first because he didn't speak English. He was different, and I was nervous. But now I'm used to him.

CARMEN: At first I didn't talk to Hassan that much. But now I talk to him more than I talk to the others.

HASSAN: My brother sleeps in the room with me. When he goes to a sleepover, I stay in Katie's bunk bed. I don't like sleeping alone. Even Jared doesn't like to sleep alone.

CARMEN: I do.

JARED: My dad makes the rules in the house. Hassan and Carmen break them.

KATIE: But Mom's the real boss.

HASSAN: Jared is the smart one; he knows practically every single animal in the world.

JARED: I want to be a paleontologist. They study fossils and stuff that's extinct, like dinosaurs and ancient mammals.

CARMEN: I want to go away to college where it's quiet. I want to be a fifth-grade teacher.

KATIE: I want to be a doctor.

HASSAN: Know what I want to be when I grow up? First, I want to be a rap man, then a football player, then a baseball player, then a soccer player. Then, I want to help poor people and be a social worker, like my dad.

HASSAN: This is a picture of me in Sierra Leone, getting ready to be adopted.

33

Jehangir: *An American President*

My last name is Hafiz. In Arabic, *Hafiz* is another name for God. I couldn't call myself Jehangir Hafiz, because that means I would be God. Instead, I call myself Jehangir *Abdul* Hafiz. *Abdul* means "servant of." I'm Jehangir, a servant of God.

I would describe my family as a very educated family interested in my well-being. There's my mom, my dad, my grandmother and grandfather from my dad's side. There's my grandfather from my mom's side—he's visiting his sister in India right now. There's my aunt, Farah, from my mom's side—I call her *Chiku*, which means "fruit" in Hindi. And last, there's me.

I have to answer to everyone. Everyone, except my aunt. She usually does the fun things with me. Everybody takes care of me and I don't have to take care of anybody 'cause I'm the youngest and the only child. I love being with lots of grown-ups.

My family's from India. People think we're Hindu because most of India is Hindu. I'm Muslim. The things I do are mostly Muslim. But the things I eat and wear are usually from Indian culture. At school, I wear casual clothes like jeans and things. If I go to a relative's party, and even at home, I wear authentic Indian clothes, called *shalwaar kamiz*, which is just a long-sleeved white shirt that has a design, and pants. It's all very loose and made of cotton.

We always eat dinner together. My mom and my aunt are the cooks, and sometimes I help. My favorite food is *achar*, a really spicy side dish that you dip your food in. There are different flavors like lemon, pickles, and stuff like that. My favorite is called *dynamite*.

I play percussion instruments: the drums, the piano, xylophone. I play football and basketball with my friends in the back-yard, but my main sport is tennis.

This picture is of me and my grandfather. He lives with us, but right now he's visiting our family in India. My grandfather is a big fan of Bill Clinton. He wants me to become the first Muslim president of the United States. He calls me "Black Clinton."

My parents expect top grades. In the last report card I had such good grades, and my parents were so proud of me. My teacher was very proud of me, so that was good.

My dream is to be the first Muslim president of the United States of America.

Eloise: *So Much to Think About*

You know what I usually think about? At least five, ten times a year? I think about what my birth parents look like and why they had to give me up. Couldn't they take care of me? Did they have other children?

I think the answer is my parents couldn't take care of me, so they left me at the gate of the orphanage in China. I feel happy because I have a very good life.

Mom and I have been together for nine years. She wishes she was nine and she kinda acts like she's ten. Mary, my god-mother, who is a very, very close friend, says it must be fun to have a mother your own age.

My mom and I both wear glasses. I like wearing them. It makes me feel I look more like Mom. Otherwise, we are very different. I'm from China. I'm interested in China and I want to see the Great Wall with Mom, but

Here I am in China, the moment I met my mom. In my baby book I wrote [well . . . actually Mom wrote it], "About 4:00 P.M., on February 12th, my mom was in her hotel room. Knock, knock. Mamma went to the door. The lady from the institute handed me to Mamma. Mamma says it was the happiest day of her whole life."

I don't feel Chinese at all. I feel 100 percent American. She's from Arkansas. She doesn't really have an accent, but whenever she gets on the phone with her dad, she'll completely change her accent. I do it, too. I say *y'all* when I talk with my cousins in the South.

If I ever have a bad day in school, my mom will say, "Please tell me." I'll say, "Do I have to tell you?" And she'll say, "No." She respects my space and I try to respect hers.

When I was three, in pre-school, my mom came to class with my baby book. I wore a red Chinese outfit that day. One of the teachers asked me, "What do you think it is to be adopted?" I said, "Adoption means you get picked up and loved."

Mom and I talk about who loves the other more. I say I love her more than life itself and she says the same. We both love each other. That's the most important thing in the whole, entire world.

ACKNOWLEDGMENTS

Many thanks to the generous families who contributed to this book:

- Hassan, Katie, Jared, and Carmen and their parents, Pat Real and Scott Auwater

- Maisie and her family, Kara Stern, John Baronian, and Erin McLaughlin

- Miriam, Asher, Leah, and Yaakov and their parents, Joy Schonberg and Richard Blum

- Noah, Megan, and Sage and their parents, Susan and Lance Chase

- Verona and Leona and their parents, Esther and Errol Gowrie

- Jehangir Abdul, his aunt Farah, his parents, Rana Arshed and Talay Hafiz, and his grandmother, Azeeza Hafiz

- Ben and his parents, Tia and Jim Harker

- Osamu and Musashi and their parents, Eriko and Nick Jacobs-Harukawa

- Joshua, Ashley, and Kati and their parents, Sy Kim and Kyung He

- Ella and her parents, Frank Marchese and Stephen McGill

- Eloise and her mom, Madge Nimocks

- Christopher, Emilio (Louie), and Adam and their parents, Marisol and David Perez

- Shareef and Aly and their parents, Ola Niessen and Mahmoud Rafeh

- Lily and Jacob and their parents, Lucy Rubin and Jennie Miller

- Kira and Matias and their parents, Lucia and Gilberto Santiago

This book is dedicated to my mother and father,
Bertha Gussman & Albert E. Greenbaum

This is a photograph of my mother, father, and me. I chose it because it reminds me of when I was six. I broke my arm climbing on pipes in the schoolyard.